Gia's New School

Story by Heather Hammonds

Illustrations by Valerie Valdivia

Contents

Chapter 1

A Move to the City

Gia and Aunt Laura had moved from the country, to live in the city.

Gia was going to start at a new school.

"I don't want to go to a new school,"
Gia said to her aunt.

Aunt Laura gave her a hug.
"You will like it, Gia," she said.

Gia went to her new room.
Aunt Laura came in.

"I liked my old school in the country,"
Gia said to her aunt.
"I had lots of friends there.
I liked the running track, too."

"You will make friends
at the new school," said Aunt Laura.

Chapter 2

A Very Big School

On Monday morning, Aunt Laura took Gia to her new school.

It was much bigger than Gia's old school.

Gia looked at all the children running around.

“This school is so big,” she said. “Where is my classroom?”

“Your teacher will show you,” Aunt Laura told her.

Aunt Laura left Gia with her new teacher.

"Here is our room," said Ms Russo.

Gia smiled. She was feeling scared, but she tried to be brave.

Gia put her bag away.
Then she went into the classroom
with Ms Russo.

Chapter 3

Gia's New Class

"This is Gia," Ms Russo said to the class.
"She is new to our school."

All the children said, "Hi, Gia!"

A girl put up her hand.
"My name is Amy," she said.
"Would you like to sit with me?"

"Yes, thank you," said Gia.

Gia looked around the classroom.
She saw lots of plants on a table.

Some of the children's work
was on the wall, too.

Gia liked her new classroom.
She started to feel better.

Chapter 4

A Walk Around the School

At lunchtime, Amy took Gia all around the school.

"Our school has a running track and a gym, too," she said.

Gia saw the school vegetable garden. There were some hens in the garden.

“I love hens,” Gia said.

After school, Gia ran out to meet Aunt Laura.

"I had a good day at my new school,"
she said.
"I think I am going to like it here!"